Richard Bentley, Edward Rud

The Diary (1709-1727) of Edward Rud

Sometime Fellow of Trinity College, and Rector of North Runcton in

Norfolk

Richard Bentley, Edward Rud

The Diary (1709-1727) of Edward Rud
Sometime Fellow of Trinity College, and Rector of North Runcton in Norfolk

ISBN/EAN: 9783744778381

Printed in Europe, USA, Canada, Australia, Japan

Cover: Foto ©Raphael Reischuk / pixelio.de

More available books at **www.hansebooks.com**

THE DIARY (1709-1720) OF

EDWARD RUD,

SOMETIME FELLOW OF TRINITY COLLEGE, AND
RECTOR OF NORTH RUNCTON IN NORFOLK;

TO WHICH ARE ADDED

SEVERAL UNPUBLISHED LETTERS OF

DR BENTLEY.

Edited for the Cambridge Antiquarian Society,

BY

HENRY RICHARDS LUARD, M.A.
FELLOW AND ASSISTANT TUTOR OF TRINITY COLLEGE, AND
PERPETUAL CURATE OF GREAT S. MARY'S, CAMBRIDGE.

Cambridge:
PRINTED BY C. J. CLAY, M.A. AT THE UNIVERSITY PRESS.
DEIGHTON, BELL & CO.; MACMILLAN & CO.
BELL & DALDY, FLEET STREET; J. R. SMITH, SOHO SQUARE,
LONDON.
1860.

PREFACE.

Edward Rud[1], whose diary is now for the first time printed, was elected Fellow of Trinity on the 2nd of October, 1701. He continued to reside in College till 1718, when he was collated by the College to the Rectory of North Runcton[2], near Lynn, in Norfolk. He had previously from 1715 to 1718 been Perpetual Curate of S. Michael's in Cambridge. Soon after his collation to North Runcton, he married Mrs. Williams, widow of Griffith Williams, his predecessor in the living. He died in 1727, leaving a valuable collection of books to the Library of Trinity College, and among them the present MS. diary.

Although copious extracts have been given by Bishop Monk, in his life of Bentley, yet there is always an advantage in having a contemporary record like the present, printed separately and *in extenso*. Its value arises from the ample details it gives of several of the most curious scenes of Dr. Bentley's history, and in the pictures of academick life as it existed a century and a half ago. Thus we find the Seniority of Trinity College discussing their

---

[1] He was entered as a sub-sizar of Trinity College, April 9, 1695, under the tuition of Mr. D. Hopkins. He is described in the admission-book as 'fil. Thomæ nat. Stogdon Episcop. Dunelm. e Schola Paulina Lond.' He became Soc. Min. Oct. 2, 1701; Soc. Maj. April 17, 1702; B.A. 1698, M.A. 1702; B.D. 1709; D.D. 1717.

[2] The advowson of North Runcton was exchanged by Trinity College for that of Reepham cum Kerdiston, in Norfolk, by means of a private Act of Parliament in 1840.

fines over the bottle, p. 15; the doctors voting in congregation in their scarlet gowns, p. 23; the proctor preventing the arrival of the musick-booths at the fair, by threatening to force them to sell in full measure, p. 4. We gain, too, several minute facts about various individuals; e.g. the disreputable conduct of Conyers Middleton, in concealing his marriage, and thus keeping his fellowship two months after it was vacant.

Of Dr. Bentley, to whom the diary owes almost all its interest, the picture that is presented is not a pleasing one. Utter want of principle and an overbearing tone and manner to all who opposed him are very manifest. And this impression is enhanced if we recollect that of the two parties into which the College was then unhappily divided, Rud decidedly belonged to the Master's —never taking any part in the prosecution, voting for him against the grace for taking away his degrees, besides assisting him in his preparations for his edition of the Greek Testament[3]. It may be added also, that Rud's character always stood high, and that he could have had no motive for giving an unfavourable colour to any of Bentley's proceedings.

The diary is written from both ends in a minute volume, which had first served some one else, and then Rud himself, as a common-place book. It contains a variety of extracts from Latin authors, hints for a method of artificial memory, extracts from books, such as Morton's *Northamptonshire*, Brown's *Travels*, Geddes's *Introduction to Vargas' Letters*, &c., with accounts of some of the books published at the time, such as Kuster's *Aristophanes* and Wasse's *Sallust*. Besides these are also 'Observa-

---

[3] See his letter to Bentley in Dr. Wordsworth's edition of R. B.'s Correspondence, p. 536. Dr. Wordsworth has expressed a doubt as to the authorship of this letter, p. 805. No one, however, could doubt, if he compared the handwriting with that of the diary. Indeed the signature 'Ed Rud.' is clear, though the E is flourished.

tions upon our old Registers', 'Excerpta out of the Audit Books of Worcester Cathedral,' a long list of ' Rents fraudulently sett by Dr. Nevile,' &c. The diary ends with the writer's marriage and settlement in North Runcton, after which it becomes literally 'a chronicle of small beer,' as four pages are filled with 'Memorandums about brewing,' giving the number of the bushels he brewed each month for two years. There is also an extract of a certificate in Chancery setting forth the extent of North Runcton glebe.

As several of the entries are scattered in different parts of the volume, I have carefully arranged them all in chronological order.

The paper drawn up by Miller against Bentley's scheme for altering the proportion of dividends of the fellows of Trinity, and the proposal for a Composition to the Master, pp. 25—27, occur in a separate part of the volume to that in which the diary is written: as also are the 'Observations on the Addresses,' pp. 27 —29, which give some interesting details of the feeling in different parts of the country after Dr. Sacheverell's trial in 1710.

The letters of Dr. Bentley which follow are all now for the first time printed. The first five were written to his future wife immediately before his marriage, and exhibit the great critick in a somewhat new aspect. The others have been obtained from the various sources indicated in the notes, and with those of Mrs. Bentley to her daughter will form a supplement to Dr. Wordsworth's collection.

I have added a few notes, and a complete index of the names of the persons mentioned. The notes might have easily been enlarged, but as all into whose hands this diary is likely to fall are familiar with Bishop Monk's admirable *Life of Bentley*, I have not repeated information to be found there. The spelling I have carefully preserved throughout, the only change I have made being that the abbreviated words are written out in full.

It is lamentable to think of the state of things in Trinity College during the time this diary was written. Bentley's marvellous powers of mind, the charm of his writings, the disreputable character of some of his opponents, and the comparative insignificance of others, have too often interested the sympathies of later times on his side. At the time, indeed, we occasionally find very strong language used respecting him, even by those who were removed from all local influence and college squabbles. Hearne's MS. Diary (of which Dr. Bliss just before his death published some extracts) affords ample instance of this[4]: and Lord Oxford, writing to Hearne, in 1731, speaks of 'that monster in nature, Bentley[5].' Although we may not be willing to go as far as this, such as have carefully studied the history of the time, and the effects his mastership had upon the condition of the College, may well echo Mr. Le Bas's prayer, "May Heaven in its mercy avert the rising of another Bentley."

For several valuable hints for the correction and illustration of the following pages I am indebted to the Rev. Joseph Edleston, Senior Fellow of Trinity College.

[4] See the extracts in Monk's *Life of Bentley*, I. p. 428, II. p. 16, note, neither of which passages is given in Dr. Bliss's *Reliquiæ Hearnianæ*.

[5] *Letters written by eminent Persons in the 17th and 18th centuries.* Lond. 1813. Vol. II. p. 86. This was just after the fire in the Cotton Library.

TRINITY COLLEGE.

August, 1860.

CONTENTS.

THE DIARY OF EDWARD RUD,
&c.

HISTORICALL MEMOIRS[1].

1709. Dr. B(entley) went to London Jan. 6, return'd the 17, 1709 expell'd Mr. Miller against the declared sense of all the Seniors on the 18, who appeal'd to the Vice Master[2] and Seniors that day. The V. Master call'd a meeting at his chambers at 9 the next morning, and that night sent the Chapple-Clerk with a written summons, in which the Master was desir'd to appear at the said meeting. But he not appearing at the time and place appointed, the V. Master and the other 7 Seniors restor'd Mr. Miller[3], and all sett their hands to their Order, viz. Stubbe, Cock, Modd, Rashly, Bathurst, Smith, Cooper, and Hanbury. By virtue of this order Mr. Miller's name was sett again upon the boards, but cutt out again presently after by the Master's order. Mr. Miller went to London the 20, and the Master on the 24. On the 26 the V. Master call'd a meeting at his chamber, where they again order'd Mr. Miller's name to be sett upon the boards.

1

1709   Feb. 4. Dr. Cressar died betwixt 10 and 11 at night very suddainly, being strangled with coughing blood.

Jan. 11. Mr. Jurin[4] sett out from hence, he gott to Newcastle on the 17, and was chosen Master of the Free-Schole and Hospitall on the 23.

Feb. 11. Mr. M(iller) exhibited a Petition against Dr. B. to the Bishop of Ely sign'd by about 30 Fellows.

Feb. 22 came on the Election of a Burghesse for Cambridge, when Mr. Sheppard had 109 votes, and Mr. Bendysh only 69.

Feb. 25. This morning the V. Master call'd a meeting, to which all the Officers were summon'd, and order'd to bring in all the books relateing to the College accounts. They were accordingly deliver'd up that day, and on the 27 the V. Master went to London.

1710. March 29. Mem: that Laurence came to me this morning, desiring to make a pair of shoes for[13]

I told him that I would give him no orders, that he was not my tradesman, but an interloper; and therefor bid him take notice that I would not be responsible for any debt contracted with him.

Sept. 4. At night Dr. Smith the Senior Dean began the custom of standing at grace, chiefly upon my sollicitation, and all the Hall readily complyed with the alteration.

5. This evening the Vice-Master return'd to College.

7. Mr. Laughton[5] the Senior Proctor hinder'd the Musick booths from coming to the fair, by threatening that he would oblige them to sell in full measure. He also reviv'd the Statute for punishing lads 3s. 4d. who came to the fair without leave under their master's hand; and on the 9 he visited Paper-mills.

14. This night Dr. Hutchinson came to College.

15. Mr. Laughton arrested the Grecian for abuseing him when he visited his coffee-booth at the fair.

22. The Master declar'd that Monday, Tuesday, and Wed-

nesday should be the days of Examination, and Friday the day 1710 of electing Fellows; and that only 7 Seniors should be present at the election, because the 8th was not yet chosen. This occasion'd a very great ferment, and his enemys seem'd mighty glad of it.

25. Dr. Stubbe, Smith, Ayloffe and Mr. Paris went to wait upon the Bishop at Ely, to desire him to proceed to the determination of our controversy; and they return'd that night.

27. Dr. B. cutt out Mr. M(iller) a 3d time.

29 was appointed for the Election of Fellows. They mett accordingly; the Master protested against 8; however 8 were sworn, and after a little quarrelling they chose only Ds. Smith senior. Mr. Middleton would have resign'd in favour of Mr. Snow, but the times being so tickleish, neither was willing to accept a conditional resignation.

30. The Seniors mett at the V. Master's Chamber to agree about all the Officers; as they did accordingly. That day Mr. Middleton resign'd absolutely, and indeed he was marryed to Mrs. Drake in August before.

Oct. 1. Ds. Snow was chosen Fellow. Some endeavours were us'd to have gott Mr. Mayor turn'd out to make room for Ds. Stockar; but as neither the Master nor Seniors were forward in it, it dropt. The Master would have chosen Dr. Smith V. Master, but the Seniors overrul'd him for Dr. Stubbe. He propos'd Dr. H(utchinson) for junior Dean, but they overrul'd him for Mr. D(rury), and indeed they had agreed on all the officers and Lecturers the night before, viz. Mr. R(ud)[6] for Lect. Prim., Mr. Bl(omer) for Lect. Græc., and Mr. Loy'd for Lect. Hum. They had taken a pique against Mr. Whit(field) for being so desirous of that office, and therefor pass'd him by, on pretence that he had one place already. Mr. C.[6] was also past by on the same account; and they also chose Mr. Pil(grim) Lect. Math. in his room. The Master acquiesc'd in all their elections, save that of Mr. D(rury).

1—2

1710   Sept. 30.   The Præcept for electing our Burghesses was read
in the Scholes, and the Thursday following, viz. Oct. 5, was
appointed the day of election.

Ditto.   Dr. Smith resign'd Chesterton, and it was declard
void in the Hall, Oct. 7.

Oct. 5.   Mr. Windsor had votes 201, Dr. Paske 149, Mr.
Shaw 93, Mr. Gill 64.   The same day Cotton and Sheperd were
chosen for the Town without opposition.

13.   This day a notable fraud was discover'd in our cellar,
the Cooper upon sounding the pipes this morning found that one
of them was quite empty, and he was ready to swear that it was
quite full on the 11th at night.   The Butler pretended a leak;
but when we went down to view it, we found the bottom of the
cask and all under it mouldy; which must all have been wash'd
away, if the pipe had run out in so short a time: but for a further proof, we order'd 3 or 4 pailes full of water to be poured into
it, and found it did not leak one drop, which was a demonstration
that the bear did not runn out at a leak.   So that it was
generally concluded that the Butler had privately conveyed it;
for it was one pipe of 4, which were the very best drink in the
cellar.   To confirm this suspicion, 2 ankers were brought to the
butterys that night to be fill'd for Mr. Bagnal of Jesus, as by
order of Mr. Hanbury and Mr. Whitfield; but upon enquiry
they both deny'd that they gave any such order; only Mr. Hanbury own'd that Mr. Bagnal had desir'd him to lett him have
a little of our bear, and he told him that if he wanted 3 or 4
gallons, they were att his service.   It then also appear'd that
Mr. Bassett having wrote to me for some of our ale, and been
refused, he found means to gett 2 ankers sett upon Mr. Baldwin's
head; they pretended Mr. Eden's order for it, but he utterly
deny'd it.   The V. Master also affirm'd that he had certain
information that some of our bear had been sold near Royston:
and I remember Dr. Smith once told me that he had been at
a feast in Suffolk, where they were served with our bread.

Oct. 26. This day came on the election of the Knights for 1710 the Shire, when Mr. Bromley had 1973 votes, Jennings 1912, Downing 1311, and Rowland 1280.

30. This time Mr. Whiston was expelled as an obstinate Heretick by the Heads, after he had thrice convented before them.

Nov. 8. Sir Nathanil Loyd was sworn V. Chancellor and made a short arch speech. But the beadles said it was contrary to form to do any other businesse on that day, being in hast to go to the collation; and he went away the next morning, having putt all the Heads into his Deputation.

10. This day Ashenhurst went out of College; whither or upon what occasion, is not known to many; but 'tis generally tho't that he designs to fly the kingdom for fear of being prosecuted for scandalous words against the Queen[7].

6. We had news brought that Mr. Mayer died on the 2d instant; but the V. Master would not declare his place void, because he durst not proceed to choose a new Senior Fellow.

13. Mr. Greenshields Master of Arts at Glascow was admitted here ad eundem gradum, ordinem et annum, demptis tribus annis. Dr. Covel V. C. dep.

16. Mr. John Reddington was marryed to Mrs. Mary Connold at Norwich.

Dec. 18 was appointed as a peremptory day by the Bishop for Dr. B. to putt in his answer to the articles; but as he had given out that he might plead his privilege as a member of the Convocation, a petition was prepar'd and sign'd in College in order to have presented to the Convocation to oblige him to wave his privilege, and Mr. Ralph Blomer, lately Fellow, was prepar'd to second it with a smart speech; to prevent which Dr. B. made applycation to Mrs. Masham (his wife is related to her husband) and by her means, upon Dr. B's exhibiting a petition complaining that the Bishop usurped the power of a general visitor, which none of his Pr-edecessors ever pretended to, and

1710 which belong'd onely to her Majesty, the Queen sent the Dr. to the Attorney General, Sir Ed. Northey, on the 12, with an order for him to inhibit the Bishop from any further proceeding 'till her majesty should be pleas'd to signify her further pleasure. Which was done, and the Attorney and Sollicitor General Mr. Raymond, were order'd to examine the Case and make their report to her majesty, whose jurisdiction the Visitation belongs to.

Jan. 2 was appointed for an hearing of this cause at Sir Edward's chamber, but by some accident it was putt of till the

4. When Mr. Mead, and Mr. Lutwich appear'd for the Master, and spent all that evening in pleading; so that the Court was adjourn'd till the

6. When Sir Peter King and Mr. Miller appear'd for the College; Sir Edward desir'd to know if there were any clause in our charter reserving a power to the Crown to give new statutes or visit. It was therefor perus'd on the 12 by Dr. Ayloffe and Mr. Cotes, who certify'd there was not such a clause.

Dec. 26 was appointed the day for voteing dividends; but when they were mett Mr. Han(bury) objected that whatever they should do before the Seniority were fill'd up, would be unlawfull and void; and he prevail'd, so that they adjourn'd to the Chapple next morning; when Mr. C(ooper) was sworn (he was chosen upon Mr. Hawkyns's death in April before), and Mr. Han(bury) was chosen to succeed Mr. Mayer. After noon they proceeded to vote ½ a Dividend for [1]708, and 2 whole ones for the 2 next years. The first moyety was paid in the beginning of January.

Jan. 9. A letter came from Miller giving an account of the hearing on the 6th, and Sir Edward's request that the Charter might be perus'd, tho' both the Master and Mr. M. assur'd him that there was nothing in it to the purpose. He also told them that he had already expended 15 guineas, and should shortly need more. They therefor ordered the Burser to send him thirty guineas.

14. News came down from Mr. Tollet that the cause before

the Attorney and Sollicitor Generall would probably be determin'd 1711
in favour of the Crown.

[1]711. July 7. Dr. B. came down to College; his wife
and children came on Thursday before.

14. It now began to be discover'd that Ashenhurst, Franke,
and Hussey had been very busy for 3 or 4 days last past in con-
triveing how to prosecute Mr. Blomer upon the 47th University
Statute, and gett him expelled for libelling the Master in the
book which he wrote against him[8].

Oct. 12. Mr. Burrell contested with Mr. Euin of Sydney
for the Rectory of Ovington in Norfolck, and lost it by one vote,
viz. 85 to 86, but Euin had 2 Nonjurors who voted for him, viz.
Mr. Baker and Mr. Billers, and tho' Mr. Burrell objected against
their votes, and desired that the oaths might be tendered to them,
yet he was over-ruled by Dr. Laney, V.C. d. and Dr. Ashton.

Nov. 12. Dr. Wright, Rector of North-Runcton near Lynn,
and Arabick Professor dyed.

19. A mandate from the Queen to make Mr. Nicholas
Saunderson, (a blind man from his infancy, but who had taught
Mathematicks in Christ's College about 4 years) Master of Arts.
It did not command, but only recommended him; and yet he
was immediately admitted and created without reading any
grace for it.

20. He was chosen Mathematick Professor in the room of
Mr. Whiston, who was expell'd for Heresy. He was oppos'd
by Mr. Hussey of Trin. Coll. and he had 4 votes; viz. Dr. Bent-
ley of Trin., Dr. Jenkins of St. John's, Dr. James of Queens', and
Sir John Ellys of Caius. But Saunderson had 6 votes, viz.
Dr. Quadringe of Magdalene, V.C., Dr. Roderick of King's, Dr.
Covell of Christ's, Dr. Ashton of Jesus, Dr. Balderston of Eman.,
and Dr. Fisher of Sydney. The rest of the Heads were not in
Town.

Jan. 21. Mr. Sanderson, the blind Professor of Mathematicks, made his inauguration speech.

1712 That day our Seniors mett, pass'd all the Audit Books, chose Mr. Cooper Pandoxator, Mr. Barwell junior Burser, and Mr. Whitfield[9] steward, and voted a whole dividend for the year ending at Michaelmas last past; and Mr. Bathurst senior Burser.

1712. Mar. 25. Dr. Roderick Provost of King's and Dean of Ely dyed this evening.

Apr. 7. This morning Dr. John Adams was chosen Provost of King's.

8. Sir Luke dyed about nine at night, and was buryed on the 12th at Abbotsleigh.

14. It was agreed by the Master and Seniors that Mr. Griffith Williams should be presented to the Rectory of North-Runcton cum Hardwick and Sechy; tho' Mr. Hacket and Dr. Bouquet both putt in for it, and were both his Seniors. But the Master sett Hacket aside, because he was not here to resign the living which he had already, tho' he was here and with the Master on the 10th, and the Seniors rejected Dr. Bouquet, because he was not naturaliz'd.

May 20. Dr. Sykes[10] hanged himself sometime this evening before candle-light in his sash, which bore his weight 'till he was dead, but broak before the morning; for he was found lying upon the floor, with part of it about his neck, the rest still hanging on the hook.

Sept. 4. Mr. Laughton[11] dyed about 6 this morning, at his niece Jenkins's house at Woodlayes near Rotheram.

16. Mr. Thoogood dyed of an atrophy.

Oct. 1. Phillip Farewell, William Birch, and Gerard Neden were chosen Fellows, William Smith junior and John Gough conducts, Dr. Smith Vice-Master, and Mr. Hanbury Senior Dean, and they were all sworn the next day.

2. Mr. Brooks of St. John's and Mr. Macrow of Caius were pricked by the Heads for competitors for the Library-Keepers-place.

3. Mr. Brooks was chosen without opposition, for Macrow

finding that almost all Trinity, Queens', and Jesus, and most of 1712 King's were against him ; soon thought fitt to give out. Brooks was prickcd by 11, Macrow by 6, Jeffries of Emanuel by 5, Paul of Jesus by 4, Burford of King's and Harris of Peter-House each by 3.

Nov. 16. This night about 10 a dreadfull fire broake out in Bottisham, which burnt very terribly, as the wind from the S. W. was very boisterous. It burnt out 22 familys, and the damage was computed at betwixt 2 and £3000.

1713. June. Dr. Hutchinson was presented to the Rectory of Chedle, tho' he was then in possession of the Vicarage of Packington, and Mr. Hacket putt by again, tho' he urg'd that statute¹² by which Dr. B. had sett him aside about a year before.

Aug. 'Twas sometime in this month, I think, that Dr. B. framed a stratagem that might have done him noteable service, if it had succeeded. The occasion of it was this. Mr. Miller saw plainly that some Courtiers, viz. Harley and Bullinbrook, were resolved to protect Dr. B. as long as they could; and therefor the inhibition to the Bishop was not recalled, tho' the Queen had ordered it about a twelve-month before. He therefor apply'd to the Queen's-Bench for a mandate to require the Bishop to proceed, or show reason why he did not. This so unexpected a power quickned the motions of the courtiers; who knew the Bishop must plead his inhibition, and they knew withall that the Queen had long agoe order'd that it should be recall'd. And therefor Bullinbrook immediately sent his letter to the Bishop to release the inhibition. Dr. B. seem'd to be all along very well pleas'd with this, and pretended that no man desir'd a speedy tryal more than he did. He therefor putt in his answer, to which Miller reply'd ; and both sides prepared for a tryal. To hasten it, he took his opportunity when Miller was in Norfolk, soon after the assizes, to propose the joyning in a petition to the Bishop to desire him to proceed to a speedy determination here in College. This hook was so nicely baited that it caught

1713 Dr. Smith, Mr. Modd, Mr. Bathurst, Mr. Barwell, Mr. Coalbatch, and 6 others: but presently after it took wind, the subtlety of it was discovered and the design blasted in 3 or 4 hours; for if the Bishop had appointed a speedy day, the Master knew very well that the accusers neither were then, nor could be ready, to make good their charge; as it would require a great deal of time to peruse all the books of accounts, which they should have occasion to make use of: and if the Bishop agreed to have it heard in College, the Master knew very well that the accusers could not be furnish'd with necessary councill. These considerations soon stop'd the progresse of the Petition. However the Master was resolv'd it should go, tho' it had but 11 hands. Accordingly Mr. Cotes carryed it to Ely. But the Bishop answered that he tho't London would be the most convenient place to try it in, both as each side might be best supply'd there with such councill as they should need, and as he also could be best furnished with assistance: that the Lord Cowper and Dr. Newton had promised to be his Assessors; and that therefor he could not certainly fix a day for the hearing, but he believ'd it would be before the Auditt, and sometime in November next.

Oct. was almost all spent in searching the College books by Miller and his friends, and taking affidavits to prepare for a tryall. About the end of the month, Mr. Miller went up with about 27 affidavits, and a great many books.

Nov. 6. Dr. B. went for London, in order to be ready for his tryall.

8. Mr. Drury dyed of an atrophy between 2 and 3 after noon: but he had made a long affidavit against Dr. B. before he dyed.

He was buryed on Friday the 16th, and this following copy of verses among others was pinn'd upon the pall; but torn of by Mr. Whitfield the Head-Lecturer at the instigation of Ashenhurst and some other of the Master's tools: it had no name to it, but was supposed to be written by[13]

Upon Mr. Drury's death.

Say, Reverend shade, what can thy labours boast,
With all thy tedious hours in study lost?
If in one moment envious fate destroys
All that youth hopes for, or that age enjoys?
Why do we grieve then at the fate of man?
Weep to behold a carcasse pale and wan?
Languid and chang'd? vain were a sigh or tear,
Did not the hoary reverend man appear,
And strike our fancys with an awfull fear.

Hail, pious shade! never shall time deface
Thy steady virtue's everlasting praise.
The same that warm'd immortall Cato's breast,
Like his was thine admir'd, like his opprest.
Like Cato fighting for his country's laws,
You stood our patriot and espous'd our cause.
As when Rome's last effort was to be try'd,
She felt her greatest losse, her Cato dy'd;
So too for you untimely lost we mourn,
Only with empty praise your herse adorn.

Untimely fate! the next revolving moon
STATUTES and LIBERTYS restor'd had shown.
That news had eas'd the bitter pangs of death,
And giv'n new vigour to thy parting breath.
One month!—with double pleasure you had dy'd,
And cry'd with Cato, Gods, I'me satisfy'd.

O for a gracious angel to inspire
My song, exalted with the Heavenly fire!
My ravish'd fancy I would raise, I'de fly
Tracing the new-blest saint i' th' yeilding sky.
I'de keep the lovely object still in view,
From seats of blisse to seats of blisse persue.

1713   There should I see, in admiration lost,
Contending saints, which should applaud him most.
Now should I stop, enamour'd of the sight,
Then rise with double vigour to the flight.
Th' illustrious shade thus happy would I trace,
And think myself most blest, when most I sing his praise.

Nov. 28. Mr. Edmund Stubbe, Fellow, marryed an Inn-keeper's daughter at Newmarket.

Jan. 18 was our Declaration day, when they voted a full dividend, and agreed to choose the officers; viz. Mr. Bathurst Senior Burser, Mr. Williams Junior Burser, Mr. Cooper Pandoxator, and Mr. Ashenhurst Steward, tho' he was absent. And yet the Master urg'd that as a reason why Dr. Stubbe was not capable of being chosen Vice master, viz. because he could not be here to be sworn the day after he was chosen.

Jan. 7. This day I began to keep my chamber, and enter into a course of physick. It soon appear'd that I had a complication of distempers upon me; viz. a violent cough attended with a dangerous asthma, and an utter depression of appetite; as also the dropsy and the inward dry piles, which last plagu'd me more than all the rest, and tormented me so very violently that I was not able to keep my bed at nights. This increas'd all the other bad symptoms, particularly the dropsy, and reduc'd me so low in about 10 days time, that my friends dispair'd of my recovery. But God be thank'd I held out till the violence of the distemper abated, and then I began to recover daily, tho' I did not return into commons till about 15 weeks after I was taken ill.

Feb. 23. Dr. Smith was taken ill suddainly on this day, whilst he was at dinner at Mr. Valavin's, and was never able to be remov'd to his chamber; for he dyed there on Saturday the 27th about 8 in the morning. 'Twas not easy to tell what he dyed of, but he had a swelling in his throat, which hindered his swallowing any sustinance; and he had a very great shortnesse of breath before he dyed. He gave the College £300 to purchase 1714 land for two Exhibitions.

1714, Mids. I now turn'd over all my pupills to Mr. Myers.

Dec. 10. Mr. Cowper dyed this morning of a lingring distemper which had wasted him almost to a skeleton. Dr. Ayloffe was chosen Senior in his room on the 18th.

[A copy of the decretory Part of the sentence against Dr. B. by Bishop Moore's directions, tho' he dyed before it was pronounced[14].]

Dec. 21. The University mett to choose a rector of Gilling in Yorkshire, it being a popish living. Mr. Gouge of Cath. Hall had 83 votes, Mr. Langley late of Jesus 61, and Mr. Stukely of Sydney 48.

Jan. 4. The University pass'd a grace to thank Dr. Bentley for writing against the Free-thinkers, and to desire him to procede in writing on that subject.

7. Mr. Pern the beadle died this night.

12. Mr. A[t]wood, Fellow of Pembroke, was chosen beadle.

13. Mr. Potter of Emanuel died of a lingring consumption, but the bell did not ring till the 14 at 10 m., for that the non-terme would have hindred the Questionists from sitting in the scholes. And therefor a convocation was called, which was turned into a congregation, and a grace passed to remove the non-term to the 3d, 4, and 5 days of February.

17, Monday. This day the Master and Seniors mett to dispose of the Vicaridge of Barrington. The Candidates were Mr. Rud[15] and Mr. Hacket; the former was Senior B.D., tho' the latter was Senior by standing. Mr. H. was himself one of the 8; and Dr. C(olbatch) who was himself personally concern'd to maintain the precedency of degrees, gain'd his point so far that Dr. B. acknowledged Mr. Rud's right, which he could not well avoid; since not only the statute, but also a conclusion[16] made by himself in interpretation of that statute [in] 1702 had determin'd that the senior by degree should have precedence in the choise of all

1714 chambers and livings, and the practise had been according to that
order ever since. But Dr. B. objected that Mr. Rud was concionator (whereas Mr. Hacket was), and that they were not obliged
to make him a concionator, that if he took this living and were not
made concionator, he must quit his fellowship, and he suppos'd
that Mr. Rud would not take it upon those terms. Dr. C(olbatch)
averred that he would. He was therefor sent for; and then
Dr. B. begun to make a long harangue to show that if any man,
that was not concionator, should take a living, he was oblig'd to
quitt his fellowship after a year. Mr. R. alledged several instances
to the contrary, as Mr. Cooper, Mr. Rashley twice, and Dr.
Hutchinson even in Dr. Bentley's own time, who all took preferment, and quitted it againe to return to College, because they were
not concionatores. However the Master insisted that itt always
had been, and always should be his rule, and that he had so much
esteem for Mr. Rud, that he could not but show him the danger he
would runn by taking that living. But Mr. Rud still insisted upon
his right. The Master urg'd that as they were not oblig'd to make
Mr. Rud concionator, so 'twas probable they would not do it if he
should take this living; and ask'd if he was willing to take it upon
that hazard. Mr. Rud reply'd that he would runn that hazard. What,
said the Master, would you take it, tho' the Seniors should declare
beforehand that they would not choose you? To which the other
answer'd that he would venture that; for he could not believe that
the majority of the Seniors would ever consent to oppresse him so
notoriously; which Dr. B. seem'd to resent, saying he tho't that
was not a proper way of argueing. Mr. Rud was then desir'd to
withdraw, and the Master (who was resolv'd to gain his point in
favour of Mr. Hacket, both as he was one of the 6 who had lately
subscrib'd a paper by which the prosecution was stop'd, and all
matters which they could not agree among themselves referred to
the Bishop of Ely, and also as he was usually one of the 8, and
therefor his vote might be of good service for the future), the
Master, I say, was forc'd to have recourse to his causa gravis-

sima; and tho' he could alledge no other cause, but that Mr. Rud 1714 was not concionator (which cause they might have remov'd as soon as they pleas'd, for Mr. Rud was ready to perform his exercise), yet he had a majority at his beck, viz. Modd, Bathurst, Hanbury, Jordan, Brabourn, and Hacket; but Dr. Ayloffe and Dr. Coalbatch oppos'd it; Modd and Brabourn alledged as their cause that Mr. Hacket was senior by standing, which was confessedly not a sufficient cause, as Dr. B. had declar'd before Mr. Rud, when he own'd that he had an undoubted right. And 'tis observable that it us'd to be a standing maxim with Dr. B. that no man ought to be chosen concionator 'till he had a collation, whereas now it seems a man's not being concionator is a sufficient reason why he ought not to have a collation.

Mar. 21. Dr. B. call'd a meeting with a design to have gott Mr. Miller cutt out; but Mr. Hanbury did not appear, as was expected, so that they did nothing but sett a little fine, and drank 2 bottels of wine: but on 23 Nat was secur'd, and therefor another meeting was call'd. Dr. A(yloffe) and Dr. C(olbatch) sent word that they were ingaged, and therefor desir'd that the meeting might be putt of. But as he had no great occasion for their presence, he sent word back that they who were not ingaged might come. Accordingly 6 of them mett, and Dr. A'yloffe, broake his ingagement to make one: which was no small surprize, and he was told that he had nothing to do there, since he had not sign'd the late pacificatory paper. However the matter was propos'd, viz. to refer Miller's case to the Bishop, and promise to acquiesce in his decision: but tho' he labour'd the matter hard and a long time too, he could not gett one man to join with him besides Mr. B(rabourn?). The next day Miller came to town, and so nothing further was done, for he was one of the 8.

1715, Ap. 11. Mem. that the great and central eclipse of the Sun, which is to happen on the 17th is calculated by Mr. Whiston so as to make the middle fall at 24 min. past 9. Dr. Halley says at 13 min. past 9, and Mr. Robert Smith T.C.C.S. says at 7 min.

1715 past 9, but I suppose he calcu[la]tes for Cambridge, whereas they
calculate for London. Observe who is nearest the truth.

July 8, circ. There was a meeting call'd about admitting the
major fellows, and Dr. B. propos'd to have Humphreys admitted
provisionally, as he call'd it. But the seniors would not allow of
that expedient; and I fancy he never design'd that it should take,
but only to draw them on to something more material. Accordingly by this means he brought them to agree that Humphreys's
right and seniority should be reserv'd to him, till the controversy
should be determin'd, and in the interim all the profitts of Miller's
fellowship should be sequestred. And this was subscrib'd by
them all; even by Ayloffe, Coalbatch, and Hacket[17]. At the same
time he prevail'd with them to make Jo. Lindsey a Beadsman,
tho' he was one of the most scandalous fellows in the whole town[18].

Mem. That the Master hath two MSS. which were given to
our library by my brother Thomas; the first about 1703, contain-
ing most of Ovid's Epistles, the 2d book of Horace's Epistles,
Persius with an interlineary glosse, St. Mathew with a glosse,
and a treatise de Institutione Scholarum, under the name of
Boetius, tho' writ by another hand. They all seem to be about
300 or 400 years old; but St. Matt. is of a clear round letter,
and may be about 200 years older. The second was sent up in
1706. It contains all Horace's Satyrs, Epistles, and Ars Poetica,
besides Persius and Ovid's Remedium Amoris. It seems to be
about 500 years old[19].

Nov. 20. Mem. That I this day began to serve the cure of
St. Michael's Parish in Cambridge.

Mem. That Dec. 13 I exhibited my own certificate[20], as also
Mr. White's, Mr. Uvedale's and Ds. Cooper to Dr. B. in order
to have them enter'd.

Jan 24. Mem. That I this day began to board with Mrs.
Thorold at dinners, being extra cōcs dim. This week I was
absent, and brought Mr. Thorold into the Hall on Candlemas day,
as also on the three first days in Shrove week. I intermitted on

Friday 17 Feb. which was therefor 3 compleat weeks; and I 1716 began again on Monday, being Feb. 27. I continu'd there 5 weeks for 30s.

1716, June 5. Mr. Roger Cotes Astronomy Professor and Fellow dyed upon a relapse into a fever attended with a violent diarrhœa and constant delirium. He was bury'd on the 9th. There were 20 rings of 20ˢ. each, and 30 at 10ˢ. each.

June 4. We begann to take down our conduit ˙in order to rebuild it.

July 16. Mr. Robert Smith, A.M. T.C.C.S. sometime agoe my pupill, was chosen Astronomy Professor in the room of Mr. Cotes.

Aug. 1. I gave the great Bible to St. Michael's Parish Church in Camb.

5. The new velvett pulpitt cloath and cushion were first used in that church; they cost £10. 10s.

7. Dr. William Fleetwood, Bp. of Ely, held his primary visitation in that church, and Mr. Hall of St. John's preach'd.

8. He confirm'd a very great multitude.

9. He visited again, and Mr. Needham of St. John's preach'd.

10. He went away, and gave me 2 guineas for the poor of my parish.

6. Mr. Martyn the Beadle dyed of the strangury.

9. Mr. Simpson of Caius and Mr. Thirlby of Jesus were prick'd for his Beadle's staff, and Mr. Thomas Day at the Bear, and Mr. Boston from Paper-mills, for the Wine License.

10. Mr. Simpson was chosen Beadle by 124 votes against 66; and tho' the choise of a vintner came on immediately after, yet there were not 100 votes on both sides; for Boston had 60 + and Day 30 +. The reason was because the University in generall seem'd to resent it very much that Mr. Scott, who had lately sett up at the Rose at a very great expense, was not prick'd,

1716 and by that means in effect utterly ruin'd; which most people
tho't was somewhat barbarous, since he was in every respect a
very civill and obligeing man, and had done nothing to deserve it;
only Mr. Shepherd us'd to lodge at his house.

Sept. 28 was appointed the day for choosing the Fellows.
Serjeant Miller was then in College, and appear'd as one of the 8.
But the Master call'd the Seniors to the Lodge first, and when
Miller enter'd with them, he had prepared a couple of constables
for his reception; who being order'd by Dr. B. threatned to turn
the Serjeant out by force, if he would not go out quietly, and one
of them actually laid hands upon him, tho' he is a Justice of
Peace for this place, and qualify'd too, which Dr. B. is not. The
Serjeant therefore went out and Dr. C(olbatch) also, declareing
against the violence that was used. But the remaining 7, viz.
Modd, Bathurst, Jordan, Barwell, Brabourn, Hackett, and Baker
proceeded to make an order[21] to deprive the Serjeant of all profits
and privileges of his fellowship 'till the suit depending between
him and Humphreys about it should be determined. They then
proceeded to the Chapple guarded by the constables, who kept
the door till all were gone in and Dr. C(olbatch) among them,
after having protested against all that had been done in his absence, and were then dismis'd with 5s. each man, and dined at the
Lodge.

They chose 5 Fellows, viz. 3 Schollars[22] and 2 Nephews, (as
the expression was, i.e. Brown, the Master's nephew, and Whitehall, Mr. Hackett's) but were overreach'd by Mr. Chichely as to
the Library-Keeper's place. It had laps'd to the Archbishop, and
Mr. C. brought down his Grace's mandate. Dr. As(henhurst)
did not like the man, and thereupon insisted mightily upon reject-
ing the mandate; which Dr. B. seem'd inclinable to do, till he
was disswaded by a wiser head, and so he was admitted.

Nov. 29. Sir John Ellis, Master of Caius College, died this
morning about 6. The Fellows chose Dr. Gouge into his place
the next day, tho' Sir John was not buryed till Dec. 3. He dyed

very rich, and yet his nephew and 2 nieces buryed him at Swaff- 1716
ham, to save charges, as was suppos'd.

Dec. 11. Dr. B. the Archdeacon held his visitation, and
Mr. Heylin[23], late of our College, preach'd a very fine sermon.

13. Mr. Sykes late of Bennet preach'd such a scandalous
sermon, with relation to the Church and Clergy, as perhaps the
like was never heard before in any place, much lesse at a
visitation[24].

Feb. In this month all the old Elms behind our Library
and on each side the walk leading to the bridge were rooted
up or fell'd, and a new walk of limes planted there. The hedge
towards the river on the south side of the bridge was then also
planted, and the walk towards Garret-Hostle lane was then
widen'd in order to be planted next year. The north hedge also,
and the hedges on each side of the terrasse or high walk were
then plash'd, and the western and part of the north ditch piled
and planked. Next year not only the south walk was planted on
each side, but also the west walk had the old hedges on each side
stubb'd up, and new ones planted.

1717. July 2d. This day Dr. B. created 9 Doctors, having
been chosen Reg. Prof. of Divinity on May the 2d before. Their
names and order were Dr. Hacket of Trin., Sherwell of Christ's,
Lovell of St. John's, Hough of Jesus, Rud of Trin., Danny of
Bennett, Uvedale and Whitfield of Trin., and Stanhope of Bennet. At the same time Dr. Warren of Trin. Hall commenced in
Law and in Physick; besides 95 A.M.

July 8. Mem. That I went down into the North, and staid
there all winter, so that I did not return to College til April
25 after.

1718. May 27. Dr. Baker and I were sent by the Master
and Seniors to wait upon my Lord Parker with a letter and a
complement from the College upon his being prefer'd to be Lord
High Chancellor, because he was formerly of our College. We
deliver'd the letter on the 29, and were invited to dine with his
Lordship on June 2d, being Whitson-Monday, and bring with us

1718 such of our Fellows as we could meet with in town. Accordingly we went about a dozen of us to Kensington, where we were entertain'd very nobly and very kindly by his Lordship till about 7 in the evening. I return'd to College on the 4th.

July 1. This day Dr. B. created 7 Doctors, viz. Dr. Hoadly of Cath. Hall, (who was one of the 30, whom the King's comeing to Cambridge in October before made Doctors all at a slapp) Dr. Boutell of St. John's, Dr. Hoddy of Magdalene, Dr. Lambert of St. John's, Dr. Warren of Jesus, Dr. St. John of St. John's, and Dr. Brookes of Caius College. Warren kept his act June 19; and I kept mine June 26. Dr. B. us'd Warren somewhat hardly in the Scholes, and therefor W(arren) who preach'd one of the Commencement sermons, took that opportunity to fall very foully upon Dr. B., at which he was very much incens'd; but he took care to be even with him in his creation speech.

July 3. I went to Norwich to visit Mr. Reddington and my other friends there. Amongst others I had the honour to dine with the Bishop on 21st, and came away the next day.

Aug. 26. This day Mr. Samuel Aubrey, Fellow of Jesus College, was found hang'd in his study, after he had been miss'd 5 or 6 days. He was near 60 years of age, but had always been look'd upon as a sort of a craz'd man.

Alderman Newton, our Auditor and Register, dy'd Sept. 22, in the morning. being near 90 years old. The two places are honestly worth about £90 per annum, (as I am told) and yet they were dispos'd of in an hurry, before the Alderman was buryed, viz. 24 inst. to Dennis Lisle, LL.B., formerly an hopefull pupill of mine, and still indebt to me; who I dare say will not lett the places sink in their value. He was sworn and admitted Oct. 2.

1718. Sept. Sometime this month Dr. Middleton gott a decree from the V. C. Dr. Goughe, to arrest Dr. B. for 4 guineas which he had extorted from the said Dr. M(iddleton) on pretence that it was his fee for an Opposition, whereas Dr. M(iddleton) being made by a Royal commencement, kept no exercise. The decree was serv'd upon Dr. B. by Mr. Clarke the Senior Beadle, 1718 who not doubting but Dr. B. would appear to the action, took no security for his appearance. But at the next Court-day nobody appear'd for Dr. B. Mr. C(larke) was therefor sent with another decree to apprehend him; but when he came to the Lodge, the Doctor lock'd himself up, and would not be seen; so that Mr. C(larke) after 3 or 4 hours stay, and no very courtly usage, was forc'd to depart without his prisoner. About this time the Chancellor came down to Newmarket, and the V. C. and Dr. Grig went to wait upon him. 'Tis not yet certainly known what their errand was, but 'tis suppos'd that it partly related to this affair, and that Dr. B. had some intelligence what pass'd there; for presently after they return'd, a meeting of the Heads was call'd; and Dr. B. being summon'd to attend by Mr. Atwood the Beadle, took that opportunity to give bail to answer Dr. M(iddleton's) action. The heads mett Oct. 3, viz. Dr. Goughe, V. C., Dr. Adams of King's, Dr. Jenkin of St. John's, Dr. Covel of Christ's, Dr. Ashton of Jesus, Dr. Laney of Pembroke, and Dr. Grig of Clare Hall (being all that were then in town save 2); but Dr. B. did not appear. The V. C. call'd for the return of his first decree, and thereupon an affidavit was read which Mr. Clarke had made, because he had the gout then and could not come abroad, wherein he gave an account of Dr. B.'s rude behaviour in this businesse, and alleged severall of his expressions in which he reflected upon the V. C. and several of the Heads; for which, and his not appearing upon summons, he was suspended ab omni gradu suscepto; and the V. C. proceeded to tell 'Lisle his Proctor that if Dr. B. did not submitt to the jurisdiction of the Court within 3 days, he would proceed to suspend him from his Professorship.

Sept. 4. Dr. B. putt in his appeal, but the V. C. doubted whether he should admitt it or not.

I find there were 2 other Heads in town, who did not appear at the Consistory; viz. Dr. Balderston of Emanuel and

1718 Dr. Richardson of Peter-House: but they had both promis'd to appear, if there should be occasion for it.

Oct. 7. There was another meeting of the Heads in the Consistory, which drew together a great conflux of people expecting mighty things; but nothing was done, save citing Mr. Brooks of St. John's, the Publick-Library-Keeper, to appear within a limited time, in order to turn him out (I suppose) for his notorious negligence. For tho' there was great occasion for his attendance, now especially whilst they are setting up the King's books in that room, which was formerly the Physick schole, yet he never came near them, nor could they tell where to find him.

9. This day being *Pridie termini*, the Professor should have preach'd *ad Clerum*, and accordingly last night he sent notice round our Hall that he design'd to do so: but the V. C. would neither suffer the bell to be rung, nor the Church door to be opened.

12. The Chancellor came over in person, din'd with the V. C. and all the Heads who were in town, approv'd of their proceedings, and determin'd that the Professor should make his submission to the persons whom he had offended. For the Professor had sent Dr. Baker with a letter to the Chancellor the day before, in which he offer'd to make a submission to him privately; but that would not do; so he went away the next day, without seeing or hearing from our Master, who did not think fitt either to go, or send, to him.

15. Another Consistory was held, when the Professor was thrice call'd for, but did not appear: whereupon his contempt was recorded, with this note under it: *Dominus deliberabit de conservanda Accademiæ Authoritate*. Thereupon the Heads went home with the V. C. and it was propos'd to degrade him absolutely by a decree; but some of the Heads not coming readily into that, it was tho't fitter to engage the body of the University in the matter. Accordingly a Grace was prepar'd for that purpose, and a congregation was call'd the next morning; but the

Master had notice of it, so Dr. Ashenhurst gott into the Caput, 1718 and by that means the Grace was quash'd; and another was propos'd that whoever shal be chosen Publick-Library-Keeper for the future shall give £500 security for the safe keeping of the books.

17. But they had taken care to secure a Caput against this day: so a congregation was call'd; and Dr. Otway of St. John's appear'd in the Caput for Law, whereupon Dr. Ashenhurst started up, and desir'd the V. Ch. to tender him the oaths; which was tho't an impertinent proposal, as by the same right he might require that the same might be done to every man in the house, which would make it an endlesse piece of work. So he was dismis'd with a reprimand; and the Grace pass'd the Caput, and was read in both houses. In the afternoon, when it was to be voted, the houses were very full, and there was the greatest appearance of scarlet that perhaps had ever been seen there in the memory of man[25]. For there were 10 Heads and 18 or 19 other Doctors. The Grace was carry'd in the Non-Regent house by 46 against 15, and in the Regent's by 62 against 35. So the late great Dr. B. was reduc'd to be a bare Harry-Soph[26], being not able to gain above 50 votes in the whole University; tho' a great many did indeed stay away that they might not offend him by voteing against him, yet 108 appear'd against him.

19. Our Master remov'd his family from All-Hallows Church to St. Michael's, because Mr. Leucas of Jesus, the Curate of All-Hallows did not vote for him, as I had done (yet he staid away) and preach'd for me himself. As he had taken care to give notice of it in the town, the Church was as full as it could well be crowded. It appear'd soon after that Mr. Lucas was really out of town at that time.

Oct. 22. I sett out for the North, and gott to Longnewton on the 27; for I rested at York on Sunday.

Feb. 23. I sett out from Longnewton and gott to Cambridge on the 27.

1719   25.   About 11 at night Mr. Edward Bathurst, A.M. a Senior Fellow dy'd suddainly, aged near 70 years.

Mar. 11.   I was presented by the College to the Rectory of North-Rungton near Lynn in Norfolk, and was instituted the next day at Ely, by Dr. Tanner, Chancellor of Norwich: I did not take Induction immediatoly; however I read the Chancellor's certificate of my subscribeing &c., and declar'd my assent to the Common-Prayer on Sunday, April 12, 1719.

[April] 16.   I return'd to College again, where I staid till

May 14, when I went back to North-Rungton to lodge at Mrs. Williams's house there: where I was received with such exceeding great civility and respect, especially by the Father and Mother, that I could not but suppose there was a meaning in it; and therefor soon began to proceed accordingly. The young widow was born May 19, 1698. I began to open a little May 18 being Whitsun-Monday.

May 30.   The young widow gave me a sort of a promise that she would marry me; but June 5, we were formally contracted *in verbis de præsenti*, before her mother.

Mem. That I was inducted June 25 by Mr. Purland, Mr. Saddleton and Mrs. Purland witnesses: and that I read the Common-Prayer and Articles on the 28th, with the same witnesses; and Mr. Towers of Christ's College was also present.

July 3.   I went from North-Runcton to Cambridge.

14.   I sett out for the North.

15.   My Father dyed and was buryed on the 17.

18.   I gott to Long-newton.

Sept. 7.   I sett out from Longnewton to Cambridge and gott thither on the 11, and Oct. 2 I went to N. Runcton.

Jan. 20.   I was marry'd at Walton to Mrs. Ann Williams, my Predecessor's widow, by Mr. James Everard, Vicar of Middleton.

As I was putt up to preach in Norwich Cathedral on May 1, my wife and I went over thither April 29 and 30; and were very kindly entertain'd at Mr. Reddington's, and by severall other 1720 friends till May 6, 1720, when we came away.

A Copy of the Paper which Mr. Miller offer'd to be subscrib'd by the Fellows Jan. 13, 1709.

We whose names are here underwritten, all of us Fellows of 1709 Trin. Coll. in Camb. do disapprove of our Master Dr. Bentley's late project of altering the proportion of our dividends, and of his excessive demands of a composition for the profitts of his Mastership, and of the unworthy and unstatuteable methods he made use of in order to compasse the same; and also of many other things done by him since he became our Master. All which, or so many of them as can be recollected and as councell shall think fitt, we desire in behalf of ourselves and the rest of the College may be represented to those who are the proper judges thereof, and in such manner as councell shall advise, humbling craving such determination and sentence therein as to the wisdom of the said judges shall seem meet.

This was subscrib'd by Dr. Stubbe, Mr. Cock, Modd, Bathurst, Rashleigh, Smith, Cooper, Hanbury, Cressar, Jordan, Drury, Barwell, Ayloffe, Welstead, Stoaks, Miller, Brabourn, Blomer, Chamberlaine, White, Craister, Middleton, Stubbe, Paris, etc.

Dr. Coalbatch scrupl'd to subscribe the Paper propos'd by Mr. Miller and therefor drew up one himself.

Whereas some disputes have lately arisen, and do still continue, between Dr. B. Master of T. C. in C. and us the Fellows of the same College, occasion'd by a certain proposall made by him the said Master for altering the proportion of our dividends, and making a composition with himself for the profitts of his Mastership; in which proposall severall particulars are contain'd, to which we cannot (as we concieve) by the Statutes of our College agree;

1709 we whose names are underwritten, the V. Master, Senior Fellows and other Fellows of the said College do, for the restoreing of peace and tranquillity to the Society, earnestly desire in behalf of ourselves and of the rest of the members of the College, that the aforesaid disputes may be referr'd to your cognizance and determination, who are the proper judges thereof, and in such manner as councell shall advise : humbly craving such sentence therein as to the wisdom and justice of such judges shal seem meet.

To a paper drawn up in these words, or to the same effect I am ready to subscribe.

J. Colbatch, T. C. C. Soc. D. D. Casuist. Professor.

Mr. Williams Senior subscrib'd also to this paper.

[This is followed by the College petition to the Bp. of Ely which is prefixed to Bentley's *Letter to the Bishop of Ely*, pp. 2—4].

When it seem'd to be agreed on all hands to allow the Master a composition, Dr. Cressar, Mr. Hanbury, Mr. Reddington and Mr. Cotes were requir'd to meet at the Lodge in order to settle it. The Master said the Fellows' statuteable commons were but £4. 6s. 8d. and produced a particular by which he show'd that they were now augmented to £32. 12s.; and because 'twas alleged that some particulars were omitted, he thought they might be sett at £34. 13s. 4d. which is 8 times their pristine value: if therefor the Master's pristine commons be sett at £80, he ought now to have

pro com.	640
pro stip. et lib. . . .	24
pro 3 equis	60
pro 3 servis	38
summa tot. . .	762

But the Master offer'd to take £700 per ann. for the whole and 1709 proportioned it as follows:

That hereafter the Senior Burser pay the Master annually

	⌠ Pro stipendio et liberatura	104
250	⎨ 3 Servants' Stip. Com. et lib.	38
	⌡ Comp. for coals, wood, charcoal, sedge, and turf .	108
100	Junior Burser for stables	100
	⌠ Steward for extra coes, Audit expens. Brawn, ⌉	
	⎪ Master's quota in festivals, pewter, linnen and ⎪	
200	⎨ furniture in moveables for the Lodge, Garden, ⎬	200
	⌡ Chandler's bills . . . . ⌋	
150	Pandoxator for bread, beer, meal, and branne . .	150
700		700

The Master and Successors to take upon them all the furniture of the two Judges' rooms, and linnen, pewter, knives, etc. for their table.

All the College goods moveable in the lodge to be valu'd by prizers, and paid for by the present Master.

This Composition to commence with the College year from Michaelmas last, and all the bread, beer, coals, etc. had since that time by the Master to be paid for by him to the College at the College rates.

OBSERVATIONS UPON THE ADDRESSES, 1710.

After the tryal of Dr. S(acheverell) the county of Gloucester first began to addresse Apr. 5. They declare for the Queen's prerogative and the Church of England, and the Protestant succession (but not Hanover) and against all republican, traiterous, factious and schismaticall opposers, and promise to chose such

1710 members as shal be affectionately dutifull etc.: introduced by the D. of Beaufort.

Then comes Cornwall Apr. 9, introduced by the Earl of Bath. They declare for the just rights of Monarchy, the Church of England, and the Protestant succession, as by law establish'd.

Apr. 5. The county of Hereford was introduced by the D. of Beaufort. They declare for loyalty, the Protestant succession, and the Church; and against those who have struck at the Royal authority and the doctrines of the Church, and promise good members.

Apr. 13. The City of London complain of daring and insolent attacks made on our institutions and republican notions infus'd by printing. They declare against antimonarchicall principles, and for the Church of England and the House of Hanover.

17. Devon, by the E. of Shrewsbury, declares for prerogative, the Church of England, and the Protestant succession; and hope they shall choose good members.

Northampton C. declares against th' encouragement of Atheism and Profaneness, for the Church, prerogative, and Protestant succession.

13. The Lieutenancy of London declare against the rebellious tumults as fomented only by Papists, Nonjurors, and such like disaffected persons; for the Queen's rightfull and lawful title, the Revolution, the Protestant succession, and the Church of England, or the Toleration.

Gloucester city declares against tumults and rebellion as the only signs that the Church was in danger, and against those who raise a clamour upon any other account; and for the Protestant succession.

Ap. 23. The County of Wilts by the E. of Shrewsbury declares against schism, faction, etc. That their professions are not occasional, that they abhor the thoughts of resisting her majesty upon any pretence, or in favour of any Pretender what-

soever (this is the first time that that string was touched) and 1710
that they will choose good members when it shal please her to
dissolve this Parliament. This is also a new stroak.

22. Warwick C. by the D. [sic] of Shrewsbury declares for
the prerogative, the Protestant succession and the Church, and
promiseth good members.

22. Warwick T. by the Lord Brook mentions dissolving
the Parliament, and promiseth to send such as will maintain
hereditary right.

24. Bath by the D. of Beaufort wonders how any one dare
to deny the Queen's hereditary right.

19. Coventry calls it undoubted hereditary right, and promiseth their endeavours to choose good members when the Queen
shall call a new Parliament.

Worcester County congratulates upon the happy suppression
of the rebellious tumults rais'd by Papists, Nonjurors, and other
enemys to the Queen's title and government.

NOTES.

p. 1. [1] The Diary begins on the reverse of the first leaf of the book.

[2] The Vice-Master was Wolfran Stubbe, D.D., who had been Regius Professor of Hebrew from 1688 to 1699.

[3] For a full account of Serjeant Miller, and his subsequent history after his bargain with Dr Bentley, see Bishop Monk's *Life of Bentley*, II. p. 87.

p. 2. [4] Of James Jurin, M.D. in 1716, there is a portrait in the smaller Combination-room of Trinity College. He was Secretary of the Royal Society.

[5] This was Richard Laughton, Fellow and Tutor of Clare Hall, a strenuous supporter of academick discipline. The statute is the 47th University Statute.

p. 3. [6] This is Edward Rud, the writer of the Diary. Mr C. immediately below, I believe to be Cotes, who was then Junior Bursar.

p. 5. [7] The scandalous words were " That the Queen was a superstitious canting woman." See Monk's *Life of Bentley*, I. pp. 261, 262.

p. 7. [8] " A full view of Dr Bentley's Letter to the Lord Bishop of Ely. In a discourse to a friend. Wherein the whole strain of that celebrated piece throughout is finally, familiarly, and largely consider'd. By Thomas Blomer, M.A. Fellow of Trinity College in Cambridge." London, 1710.

p. 8. [9] This is an error. Mountagu Lloyd was elected Steward on this occasion.

[10] Dr Sike had been made Hebrew Professor through Bentley's influence in 1705. See Monk's *Life of Bentley*, I. pp. 186, 329. The rooms in which the suicide was committed are those next the Library on the south side of Neville's Court. See Wordsworth's *Correspondence of Bentley*, p. 785.

[11] This was John Laughton, or Lawton, "a great personal friend of Sir Isaac Newton and Charles Montague. He was afterwards Librarian and Chaplain of Trinity. He subsequently became Canon of Worcester and Lichfield, and gave to the Library of Trinity College a valuable collection of books." Brewster's *Life of Newton*, II. p. 191, note 2.

p. 9. [12] This is Statute 30, *De Sacerdotiorum collatione.*

p. 10. [13] Thus left blank in the original.

p. 13. [14] This will be found in Monk's *Life of Bentley*, i. p. 365.

[15] Rud, the writer of the Diary, was A.B 1698, A.M. 1702, B.D. 1709. Hacket was A.B. 1691, A.M. 1695, B.D. 1710.

[16] Extract from Trin. Coll. Conclusion Book :—

June 3, 1702.

" Whereas a dispute arose among several fellows of the College about the meaning of these expressions in the 26 and 30 statutes, *Seniori secundum suum gradum*, and *Secundum gradum marime seniori:* Agreed and determined by the Master and Seniors, that the true meaning thereof is, that all Batchelors of Divinity have the prælection of College Chambers and College livings before all Masters of Arts ; and that one Batchelor of Divinity have the præoption before another according to the Seniority of admission to the said degree in the University."

Ric. Bentley, Mag. Coll.

p. 16. [17] Extract from Trin. Coll. Conclusion Book :—

July the 8th, 1715.

" Whereas David Humphreys now Master of Arts was lately by Master and Seniors chosen minor fellow conditionally upon the supposition that Mr. Miller's fellowship then under controversy was declar'd void by the time of next admission to major fellowships; and now the said time of admission is come, the said controversy lies yet before his majesty undetermind: Agreed by the Master and Seniors, that if the royal determination (when given) be for the nullity of the said Mr. Miller's fellowship, the said David Humphreys shall be forthwith admitted into it: and that in the mean time all profits of the said fellowship be reservd in the College hands, till it shall be known to whom they are due."

Wᴹ. Ayloffe.	Ri. Bentley.
J. Colbatch.	Geo. Modd.
J. Hacket.	Edw. Bathurst.
Jᵒ. Baker.	Abra. Jordan.
	Matt. Barwell.

[18] Lindsay had been the leader of the Tory mob at the late election. See Monk, i. p. 391.

[19] These MSS. now are marked R 3, 18, and R 3, 29, in Trin. Coll. Library. They both shew traces of Bentley's use of them. The second contains several treatises besides those mentioned. The scribe has dated one of them, a treatise contra Hæreticos, by Alanus de Monte Pessulano, Paris, 1219, which is about the date of the whole volume.

[20] This entry is written on the first leaf of the book, separate from the rest, with no mention of the year. It probably refers to the certificates of

having taken the oaths to George I. in 1715. In the next paragraph *extra coes dim.* means that he had for this first week of his absence from hall the allowance for extra commons for half the week, given in cases of illness.

p. 18. [21] Extract from Trin. Coll. Conclusion Book :—

Sept. 28, 1716.

"Whereas by a conclusion made July 8th, 1715 the right and title of a fellowship of this College then lying between Mr Miller and Mr Humphreys, and referrd to his Majesties determination : it was orderd by Master and Seniors, That all profits of the said fellowship be reserved in the College hands, till it shall be known to whom they are due ; and whereas the said Mr Miller pretends even before his Majesties answer is receivd to claim the profits and power of a fellow : It is resolvd and orderd by the Master and Seniors, that neither the said Mr. Miller nor Mr. Humphreys, till his Majesties determination be given, do in any regard whatever act as a fellow of this College."

Agreed to the order above written:

Rich. Bentley.
Geo. Modd.
Edv. Bathurst.
Abra. Jordan.
Matt. Barwell.
Ja. Brabourn.
J. Hacket.
J⁰. Baker.

[22] The 'three Schollars' were Leonard Thomson, Zachary Pearce, and John Walker. See Monk's *Life of Bentley*, I. p. 411.

p. 19. [23] John Heylyn, or Heylin, was Prebendary of Westminster, Rector of S. Mary-le-Strand, London, and the author of *Theological Lectures to the King's Scholars at Westminster Abbey*. London, 1749, &c. He was a fellow student of Sir I. Newton's nephew, Conduitt, at Trinity. See Brewster's *Life of Newton*, II. p. 397, note 2.

[24] "The difference between the kingdom of Christ and the kingdom of this world; set forth in a sermon (on S. Joh. xviii. 36 preached at the Archdeacon's visitation in S. Michael's Church in Cambridge, Dec. 13, 1716. By Arthur Ashley Sykes, M.A. Rector of Dry-Drayton, near Cambridge." See an account of the sermon in Disney's Life of Sykes, p. 42.

p. 23. [25] This scene took place in what is now the North room of the University Library, where the Catalogue is kept.

[26] i. e. ἐρίσοφος, a person who has kept all his terms, but who is without a degree.

LETTERS OF DR. BENTLEY AND HIS WIFE.

I.[1]

Dr. Bentley to Mrs. Johanna Bernard.

TRIN. *Sept.* 5, 1700.

HONOURED MADAM,

I SHOULD have made bold either to have written to you, or have waited on you before this time, if Mr. Brown's last letter had not hindered me, which gave me hopes, that within a short time after the date of it he would be at Cambridg, where he would discourse the affair at larg. But it seems, some Company in his family detained him from his intended visit till yesterday, when I had the happiness of seeing him here, and of debating with him concerning the subject of his last letter. I have laid before him my real thoughts about it, which (after the best examination I am able to make) appears to me to be the greatest advantage for you, as well as, and even more than for myself. If what he shall represent to you is not enough to give you satisfaction, I hope before you determine any thing finally, you will please to take the opinion of some persons that are competent Judges in a thing of this nature, which is not to depend on common

3

examples, but upon reason and prudence: or that you will please
to give me myself leave to lay before you my own reasons; if
perhaps I may be so happy to gain any credit with you. I beg
leave to present my humble service to Mrs. Lucy with a thousand
thanks for her last letter.

I am, Honoured Madam,

Your most faithfull and affectionate servant,

R. BENTLEY.

For the Honoured Mrs. Johanna
Bernard at Arlesey in Bed-
fordshire.

II.

Dr. Bentley to Mrs. Johanna Bernard.

LONDON, Nov^{ber}. 13th, 1700.

MY DEAREST FRIEND,

BEING to take leave of the town to morrow morning, I
cannot spend some of the remaining minutes more pleasantly,
than in conversing with my dearest. For while I am writing to
you, methinks I see you and speak with you, and from thence
receive a great satisfaction and increase of my love. To speak
the truth, since I thought I might safely reckon you my own, I
have given all the scope to love, and let it increase without reserve
or restraint; so that I now find myself quite another man, and so
engaged in affection to you, that my happiness and quiet is absolutely in your power. Pray do you the like on your part; and do
not keep all affection under the curb; but begin to love now,
whome, when your duty obliges you to it, you will never think

you love too much. If it be possible I will leave Cambridg and return hither in 9 or 10 days: and do not tell me, as you did while I was with you, that that will be too soon: for love makes every week seem to me a month. I hope then to find you still in Berkshire, and to wait on you from thence to London: where several of my Friends the Bishops will be then ready and willing to join us together. I leave the management of the Coach and other matters to Mr. P(edley) and yourself. What you approve of, shall be done. I have said nothing yet to my Lady B(ernard) nor shall I see her again, before I go. And I believe it's better not take Arlesey in my way now to Cambridg, because you yourself have given them an account by Letter. Pray God preserve you in health and ease of mind; and in all other things I trust you will ever find me

Your most affectionate humble servant

R. B.

For Mrs. Bernard at Mrs. Palmer's House near Ockingham in Berkshire.

III.

Dr. Bentley to Mrs. Johanna Bernard.

LONDON, Nov^{er}. 23, 1700.

MY DEAREST FRIEND,

SINCE I had the pleasure of writing my last letter to you, I have been at Cambridg, and enterd upon my Vicechancellorship; and have had as happy a stay there, as I could expect in the absence of a person who has engaged all my affection. When I had settled affairs so there, that I might be spared for about ten days, I immediately took horse for London, and arrived here to

3—2

day at 12 a clock. I made it my first business to find out Mr.
Pedley to hear news of my dearest's precious health; and with
him I found a letter of yours mixd with several tokens of kindness, which I wish you a thousand blessings for: there is one
scruple you renew again, though you was pleasd, as I took it, to
lay it aside, after it had been named, when I was with you.
Mr. Dobyns cannot be found to night, and so I cannot give you
an account of his judgment about it. Beleeve me, if it was truly
for your honor or your ease to have such a condition, I should be
the first that offerd it; but I question not, but upon riper thoughts
you will think it more becoming your character to wave it, and to
trust Providence with such an event, rather than fence against it
by such means, as will make you look like a very hard hearted
mother. But I do not here argue the matter with you; I will
take the first occasion of seeing you, and then I hope you and I
shall end it to the content of both. I must take the Oaths at
Westminster Hall on Monday morning to qualify me as Vicechancellor. I was pleasd with the thoughts of returning back to
Cambridg in ten days time a happy Husband: this delaying
scruple makes me spend my time melancholy. But the comfort
is, I hope it will be soon over, for assure yourself, I shall never
deny you anything, that I can beleeve in my conscience is for
your real advantage and reputation. Adieu, my sweetest love,
and beleeve that in your kindness is folded up the main happiness
of your affectionate humble servant

R. BENTLEY.

For Mrs. Johanna Bernard at
Mrs. Palmer's House near
Ockingham in Berkshire.

37

IV.

Dr. Bentley to Mrs. Johanna Bernard.

TRIN. COLLEGE,
Dec. 12, 1700.

MY DEAREST LOVE,

I RECEIVD a letter of yours to Mr. Pedley, giving him reasons why he should stop my coming to London till Christmas: I am extremely sorry (more than if I felt them myself) that the Toothach and Cold with a little Deafness are among those reasons. I am more sensibly touchd with any thing that befalls you than if myself was the sufferer. But with submission I cannot take that for a good reason, why I should put off my journey : for surely on such occasions my presence is the most due, to comfort you and assist you, to nurse and to cherish you. Neither has your other reason, that I shall be better humord after my sermon's over, any great force in it. For when you are kind, I dare say I can be good humord in any condition. Besides, I could have assignd that course of preaching to another person, and so I had not been obliged to return so soon again to Cambridg. However there are some other reasons you mention, and chiefest of all your own desire and command (which I shall always study to comply with, if it be consistent with your own good) that have made me content to stay here till Christmas day is gon. But then my judgment, and request is, that you would be at London, and let us have the honour of being married by some Bishop. You may have your cloths in readiness by that time; and I will leave Cambridg so as to be at London to be married on New Years day. I have many reasons to make choice of that day. Tis the first day of this new Century, tis the day I first came to Br. Stillingfleet², tis the first day of my Birth-month; and I hope it will be an omen of prosperousness and felicity. For God's sake then, my sweetest Love, comply with me in this, and let me hear it from yourself, that I shall find you then at London without further delays of my hopes; for as you say well, it does not become my character and station to fly backwards and forwards, especially without concluding my great affair. My service to Mr. Pedley and Mrs. Palmer. God bless and preserve you. Pray do not fail to let me have a letter from you.

For Mrs. Bernard at Mrs. Palmer's
House near Ockingham in Berkshire.

V.

Dr. Bentley to Mrs. Johanna Bernard.

SATURDAY NIGHT.
St. James's.

MY DEAREST LOVE,

I CAME hither this night from Cambridg, and immediately sent to my Lady Bernard's to know if you was come thither, or if not, whether you had writ to her about your coming. But I was surprizd and troubled to know by her, that she had no notice at all from you. But still my hope is that you design to come for London on Monday night next. For you know that in my last I was content upon your desire that we should deferr our affair till after Christmas day; but that for many reasons I entreated you to pitch upon New Year's day, and to be in London, that we might be married by a Bishop or the Archbishop[3]. This I took was granted; for though I could not obtain the favour I wisht of knowing it from your own hand, yet Mr. Pedley promised it in a letter of his, and I supposed not without your knowledge and leave. Accordingly, I despatcht affairs at Cambridg, and have a month here at command; I came up [by] the stage coach, thinking certainly to find you here ; and have no riding cloths here nor my horses. So that upon all accounts both of love, discretion, and mere necessity, I must entreat you to come to Town, and finish this affair here. My character and office of Vicechancellor makes all my motions so public and taken notice of, that I cannot do what I should be willing to if I acted privately. The common news at the University was, that the Licence was out a month ago, and that New Years day was fixd upon for the day. How they had these stories, God knows; neither of them could come from me, for I spoke to no soul about them. So that if you will follow nothing but that general Rule, that it's decent for the Lady to be as backward, as she can make excuses for ; you will make me ashamed to shew my face here in the Town. For I shall see no body, but they will be wishing me Joy. But I hope the other way, that you will rather be governd by particular occasions, than by humdrum general Rules ; and then I am sure you will be here before New Years day : unless some illness (which God forbid) should prevent it. Mrs. Burnet is in Town here, but I stirr not abroad to night. My service to Mrs. Palmer : God keep thee well, my dearest Life ; though I myself shall not be well, till I either hear from you, or see you here. Adieu.

Y^r most affectionate,

R. B.

*For Mrs. Bernard at Mrs. Palmer's
House near Ockingham in Berkshire.*

VI.[4]

Dr. Bentley to Mr. Leeds[5].

DEAR SIR,

I UNDERSTAND by Mr. Knight[6], that the gentleman requires such a tutor for his son, as does not design to take Holy Orders for three years. And that for this reason he has left off all thoughts of the place, being both disposed in his own judgment, and advised by his friends to enter into Priest's Orders, as soon as occasion offers. I beg leave therefore to recommend another of this College to be tutor to the gentleman's son in room of Mr. Knight. He is of the year above him, and is son to Dr. Wright our Arabic Professor. I had a thorough examination of him, when he was candidate last September for a fellowship; and can pass my word for his abilities not only in Greek and Latin, but Philosophy, Geography, Geometry, History, &c. so that he is every way well qualified for the place he now desires. If there had been one fellowship more void, I believe it would have faln to his share. And in short, I am persuaded the gentleman will hardly meet with another so well accomplishd for his purpose, as he is. You will pardon this trouble, which I could not but give you, as well at the request of Dr. Wright, as out of my own esteem and concern for the young man[7].

I am, Sir,

Y^r humble servant,

RI. BENTLEY.

Jan. 29, 170⅔.

For Mr. Leeds at Bury
in Suffolk.

VII.[a]

Dr. Bentley to the Rev. Mr. Posthlethwait.

DEAR SIR,

My nephew[9], when he was last here, made such improvement of his time under the assistance of Dr. Sike and others, and gave such a specimen of his studiousness and discretion, that I was much pressed by several of the College to admit him then: but that I was unwilling to do having not acquainted you with it: but agreed, that considering he was now 16 years of age, and would be capable of Orders by the time of commencing Master of Arts, and gaining so promising a prospect of good behaviour here, he should be admitted at Christmas next. I desire therefore you would send him hither, as soon as you break up for the Holidays; and all accounts with you, if they are not settled before, shall afterwards, when I see you about February, be adjusted by your

Affectionate humble servant,

RI. BENTLEY.

I am glad to hear that Betterly[10] is to go to Worcester, and he'll have here, S[r] Smith, a very good scholar and goodnatured discreet young man, for his usher; so that they can hardly fail of raising the reputation of that school.

TRIN. COLL.
Nov. 20, 1707.

Addressed

For the Rev. Mr. Posthlethwait,
Master of St. Paul's School
in London.

VIII.[11]

Dr. Bentley to Dr. Stubbe.

DEAR SIR,

I THANK you for your letter, and particularly am glad that my nephew deserves your good opinion. I have not spoken to any one to preach at the beginning of the term, because as I leave the authority of the Master with you in my absence, so I leave the onus too that is contingent during that absence. And this is agreeable to all ancient custom in the College. So that you must contentedly take your share of the burden as well as the honour, and if you do not put up a friend, you will do well (as you say) to carry a sermon in your pocket. I like your resolution about the affair of Mr. Laney, and remain, Sir,

Your affectionate friend and servant,

R. BENTLEY.

Jan. 27th, 1708.

Addressed

For the Rev. Dr. Stubbe, Vice-Master of Trinity College, Cambridge.

IX.

Mrs. Bentley to Mrs. Cumberland[12].

March the 27th [1732].

MY DEAR CHILD,

WE as well as you, was surprized at Mr. Ridges going for he had not spoke of it to us before he was just a going. I know not whether we shall go to London or not. I think 'tis better staying because neither Dr. Bentley's health nor inclinations incline him to visit and 'tis better staying at home here than in Lodgings. He and Dr. Walker[13] went on Monday morning to Fullborn to try how the Air would agree with him; we think he has eatt better since, and my head is much better, tho' not quite well. I think you had the receit Miss Patrick wrote; but it being entered in my Book, I here send it you. To make Ratefea Biskets. Take a quarter of a pound of Apricoks kernels or bitter Almonds, an equal quantity of sweet Almonds; blanch them, and beat them very well with 3 spoonfull of Rose water and 3 of fair water, beat 9 eggs leaving out the whites of 4, by degrees put in a pound of Loaf Sugar finely sifted, then beat it an hour before you put in the Almonds when 'tis mixed stir in 8 ounces[14].

The letters are come and I dont find 'tis necessary for Dr. Bentley to go to London; my niece Malabar goes on Monday next and designs to call upon us, for she must go through this town. I am allmost tyred with writing so will only give my Service and Love and assure you that I am

Your sincerely affectionat Mother,

J. BENTLEY.

Dr. Hackett is come to be ready to go or stay here as will be found most convenient.

expence of Mr Tinkler; but, even with this enlargement of the building, there is not more than sufficient accommodation for the village school, and for the residence of the schoolmaster and schoolmistress. The premises are kept in order by the rector; who, also, as well as the college, and Worts' trustees, contributes liberally to the necessary school fund.

In the parish are two double cottages. One of them, that to the south of the clerk's house, it has been agreed to consider as Badsley's charity. By an order of the present Charity Commissioners, dated 11th June, 1861, it is eventually to be pulled down, and the ground, on which it stands, to form the site for a new school-room. The other, to the north of the clerk's house, is supposed to have been the widow Hutton's. This is likewise to be taken down, when some substantial cottages will be built in its place, the proceeds from which are to go, by direction of the same authorities, towards the maintenance, and repair, of the fabric of the church. The rector and churchwardens in the first case, the churchwardens alone in the second, to be in future the trustees of the property, which has hitherto been managed according to the decision of a vestry-meeting held 8th November, 1850.

A trust has always existed in the parish for the management of some, if not of the whole, of the land left in Roman Catholic times to the church. The earliest document connected with it is one, by which Adam Clerke, the rector, transferred, 24th August, 1 Edward IV. [1461], to Thomas Clerke, John Clerke, clergyman, and Thomas Wodward, chaplain, two acres of arable land. He had himself been a trustee of this land, and of other lands belonging to the parish, in conjunction with John Hacche lately dead, having been appointed by Thomas Brooke, chaplain. The witnesses to the deed are Henry Lane, William Chamberlayne, John Fen, Richard Hacche, and John Scotte. Henry Lane, and Henry Gararde, delivered over the same land, 28th February, 20 Edw. IV. [1481], to John Bedenham. These two had had for their co-trustees Henry Wentworth of Nettylstead[1], armiger, William Foorthe of Colcestia (Colchester), and Thomas Thyes of Cambridge, clergyman, all dead ; and they had succeeded John Clerke lately of Landbeach, clergyman, and Thomas Clerke. The sealing of this document was witnessed by John Wryght, Walter Mascall, John Grene, Robert Sockelynge, and John Watkyn. Thomas Warde senior, son and heir of Roger Warde recently deceased, created a new trust, 4th December, 2 Elizabeth [1559], in favour of Master John Porye, D.D. rector, Henry Gotobed, yeoman, Nicholas Aunger, Richard Thurlowe, Thomas Warde junior, John Hacche, and William Lane. The land, however, is at length stated to be four acres, and the phrase simul cum aliis terris is omitted, as well as the names of Thomas Warde's co-trustees, and of those whom he succeeded in the trust. The trust land continued to be conveyed in a similar manner down to a very recent period. Since the Reformation, (whatever may have been the case previously,) it is probable, that the profits arising from this land were always applied, as they are now, to the general expences of the church. For, in the churchwardens' accounts from 1639 to 1681, we invariably find a sum of money added, as received for rent of the town land.

These churchwardens' accounts exhibit another item — received from the Church Lotte ; and this item, which has not occurred, and which could not occur, subsequently to the inclosure of the parish, is thus to be explained. Frith fen[2] was entirely grass land, and was laid out afresh every year among those persons, to whom certain portions of it belonged. The measurement was made throughout ' with a pole of xiij foot in

[1] Margaret, daughter of Sir *John* Wentworth of Nettlestead in Suffolk, married Sir John Seymour of Wolf Hall in Wiltshire, and became the mother of Jane Seymour, third queen of Hen. VIII.

[2] The ditch lying on the north quarter of Frith fen was called Landbeach Tilling. The water ran from this into the fens by means of another ditch styled Lode ditch, and so on, probably, to the Old Ouse.

NOTES.

p. 33. [1] This and the following four letters, written by Dr. Bentley to his future wife, immediately before their marriage, are in the possession of the Rev. W. R. Ick, late Fellow of Sidney Sussex College, and Vicar of Peasemarsh, a descendant of Mrs. Cumberland, by whose kind permission they are now printed.

Mrs. Johanna Bernard, the lady, was the daughter of Sir John Bernard of Brampton in Huntingdonshire. See Monk, i. p. 151.

p. 37. [2] In 168$\frac{2}{3}$. He was born Jan. 27, 166$\frac{1}{2}$.

p. 38. [3] They were married on Jan. 4, at Windsor, by Dr. Richardson, Master of Peter-House.

p. 40. [4] From a collection of Mr. Leeds' correspondence, now in the Library of Trinity College, purchased at the sale of the late Dawson Turner, Esq., of Yarmouth.

— [5] Edward Leedes, who for 40 years was master of the Free Grammar School at Bury St. Edmund's, died Dec. 20, 1707, in the 80th year of his age. He published *Methodus Græcam linguam docendi*, Lond. 1690, and *Luciani Dialogi*, Cant. 1704, frequently reprinted since.

— [6] This was Samuel Knight, B.A. 1702, A.M. 1706, D.D. 1717, afterwards Prebendary of Westminster, Author of the Lives of Erasmus and Dean Colet.

— [7] The application was not successful, as the place was filled up before this letter was received, by a son of Mr. Leedes himself.

p. 41. [8] In the possession of the Rev. R. E. Kerrich, of Christ's College, by whose permission it is printed. Posthlethwait was Master of St. Paul's School in London.

— [9] This was Thomas Bentley, afterwards fellow of Trinity, editor of the 'little' Horace, Callimachus, and Cæsar's Commentaries.

— [10] Betterley was a Bachelor of Arts of Trinity, B.A. 1705, M.A. 1709. The Smith mentioned in the next line is possibly Edward Smith, B.A. 1707, afterwards Fellow.

p. 42. [11] This letter was formerly in the possession of Dawson Turner, Esq.

p. 43. [12] These two letters of Mrs. Bentley to Mrs. Cumberland, her daughter, are in the possession of the Rev. W. R. Ick.

— [13] Richard Walker, afterwards Vice-Master of Trin. Coll.

— [14] The letter is torn here.

p. 44. [15] This was the appeal from the decision of the King's Bench to the House of Lords. See Monk, II. p. 326.

— [16] Mrs. Ridge, Bentley's elder daughter, wife of Humphry Ridge, Esq. After his death she married the Rev. James Favell, a fellow of Trinity.

INDEX OF PERSONS.

4

Laughton, Richard, Fell. of Clare Hall, 2.

Laureuce, a bootmaker, 2.

Leeds, Edward, Master of Bury School, 40.

Lucas, John, Fell. of Jesus, 23.

Lindsey, Joseph, 16.

Lisle, Dennis, Trin. Hall, 20. 21.

Lloyd, Mountagu, Fell. of Trin. 3. 8 (note).

Lloyd, Sir Nathaniel, Master of Trin. Hall, 5.

Lovel, Edward, Fellow of S. John's, 19.

Lucy, Mrs. 34.

Luke, John, Trin. 8.

Lutwich, Mr. 6.

Macrow, Thomas, Fell. of Caius, 8. 9.

Malabar, Mrs. 43.

Marlborough, Duke of, 45.

Martyn, Hugh, Fell. of Pemb, Esquire Bedell, 17.

Masham, Mrs. 5.

Mayor, William, Fell. of Trin. 3. 5. 6.

Mead, Mr. 6.

Middleton, Conyers, Fell. of Trin. 3. 20. 21. 25.

Miller, Edmund, Fell. of Trin. 1. 2. 6. 9. 10. 15. 16. 18. 25.

Modd, George, Fell. of Trin. 1. 10. 15. 18. 25.

Moore, John, Bp. of Ely, 2. 3. 5. 9. 10. 13.

Myers, John, Fell. of Trin. 13.

Neden, Gerard, Fell. of Trin. 8.

Needham, Peter, Fell. of S. John's, 17.

Newton, Alderman, 20.

Newton, Dr. 10.

Northey, Sir E. 6.

Otway, Charles, Fell. of S. John's, 23.

Palmer, Mrs. 38. 39.

Paris, John, Fell. of Trin. 3. 25.

Parker, Lord Chief Justice, 19.

Paske, Thomas, Fell. of Clare Hall, M.P. for the University, 4.

Patrick, Miss, 43.

Paul, George, Fell. of Jesus, 9.

Pearce, Zachary, Fell. of Trin. 18 note (p. 32).

Pedley, Mr. 35. 36. 37. 38.

Pern, John, Fell. of Pet., Esquire Bedell, 13.

Pilgrim, Thomas, Fell. of Trin. and Prof. of Greek, 3.

Postlethwaite, John, Master of S. Paul's School, 41.

Potter, Edward, Fell. of Emman. 13.

Purland, Mr. 24.

Purland, Mrs. 24.

Quadringe, Gabriel, Master of Magdalen, 7.

Rashleigh, Nathaniel, Fell. of Trin. 1. 14 25.

Raymond, Sir Robert, Attorney-General, 6.

Reddington, John, Fell. of Trin. 5. 20. 25. 26.

Richardson, Thomas, Master of Pet. 22. 46.

Ridge, Humphry, Trin. Hall, 43.

Ridge, Mrs. 44.

Roderick, Charles, Provost of King's, 7. 8.

Rowland, David, 5.

Rud, Edward, Fell. of Trin. 3. 12 13. 14. 15. 16. 19. 20. 23. 24.

Rud, Thomas, Trin. 16.

Sacheverell, Dr. Henry, 27.

Saddleton, Mr. 24.

Saunderson, Nicholas, Christ's, Lucasian Professor, 7.

St John Pawlet, Fell. of S. John's, 20

Scott, Mr. 17.

Shaw, William, S. John's, 4.

Shepherd (Sheppard), Samuel, M.P. for Cambridge, 2. 4. 18.

Sherlock, Thomas, Bp. of Bangor, 44.

Sherwell (Sherwill), Thomas, Christ's, 19.

Shrewsbury, Earl of, 28. 29.

Simpson, Robert, Fell. of Caius, Esquire Bedell, 17.

Smith, Edward, Fell. of Trin. 3. 41 (note).

Smith, Robert, Fell. (afterwards Master) of Trin., Lucasian Prof. 15. 17.

Smith, Thomas, Fell. of Trin. 1. 2. 3. 4. 8. 10. 12. 25.

Smith, William, Trin. 8.

Snow, Matthew, Fell. of Trin. 3.

Somerset, Duke of, Chancellor of the University, 21. 22. 44.

Stanhope, Michael, Benet, 19.

Stillingfleet, Edward, Bp. of Worcester, 37.

Stoaks, Richard, Fell. of Trin. 25.

Stockar, Peter, Trin. 3.

Stubbe, Edmund, Fell. of Trin. 12. 25.

Stubbe, Wolfran, Fell. of Trin., Prof. of Heb. 1. 2. 3. 4. 12. 25. 42.

Stukely (Stucley), Peter, Fell. of Sidney, 13.

Sunderland, Lord, 45.

Sykes, Arthur Ashley, Benet, 19.

Sykes (Sike), Henry, Prof. of Hebrew, 8, 41.

Tanner, Thomas, Chancellor of Norwich, 24.

Thirlby, Styan, Fell. of Jesus, 17.

Thomson, Leonard, Fell. of Trin. 18 (note).

Thoogood, Mr. 8.

Thorold, Mr. 16.

Thorold, Mrs. 16.

Tollet, George, Fell. of Trin. 6.

Towers (Samuel, Joh. ?), 24.

Trevor, Miss, 45.

Trimnel, Charles, Bp. of Norwich, 19.

Uvedale, Robert, Fell. of Trin. 16. 19.

Valavin (? Vallavine, Peter, of Peter House), 12.

Wake, William, Archb. of Canterbury 18.

Walker, John, Fell. of Trin. 18 (note).

Walker, Richard, Fell. of Trin. 43.

Warren, Richard, Fell. of Jesus, 20.

Warren, William, Trin. Hall, 19.

Wolstead, Ralph, Fell. of Trin. 25.

Whiston, William, Fell. of Clare, Lucasian Prof. 5. 7. 15.

White, Samuel, Fell. of Trin. 16. 25.

Whitehall, James, Fell. of Trin. 18.

Whitfield, John, Fell. of Trin. 3. 4. 8. 10. 19.

Williams, Mrs. Ann, 24.

Williams, Griffith, Fell. of Trin. 8. 26.

Williams, John, Fellow of Trin. 12.

Winchelsea, Lord, 44.

Windsor, Dixie, Fell. of Trin., M.P. for the University, 4.

Wright, Charles, Fell. of Trin., Prof. of Arabick, 7. 40.

Wright, Robert, Trin. 40.

CAMBRIDGE: PRINTED AT THE UNIVERSITY PRESS.